Minnie the Mule and the Erie Canal

BOOK ONE

by Lettie A. Petrie

Illustrated by Beth Petrie

Additional Titles By Author

ADIRONDACK FAIRY TALES
1997

Coming Soon
A BAKER'S DOZEN
Erie Canal Series Book Two

Minnie The Mule And The Erie Canal
By Lettie A. Petrie
Copyright © 2001

Illustrated by Beth L. Petrie
Westdale, New York 13483

Printed in the United States of America
by Patterson Printing, Michigan

Library of Congress Cataloguing-in-Publication Data

CIP applied for

ISBN 0-9711638-04

Published By
Petrie Press
9 Card Avenue
Camden NY 13316

Minnie the Mule and the Erie Canal

by Lettie A. Petrie
Illustrated by Beth L. Petrie

For My Family
Who Makes All Things Possible

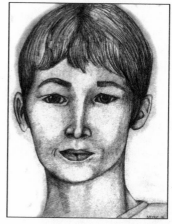

JACK

SARAH

MINNIE THE MULE

ALL ABOUT
Minnie the Mule and the Erie Canal

One-hundred-fifty years ago, Minnie the Mule worked for Captain John Fairweather's family on the busy Erie Canal. The Canal went east from Rome, New York to New York City. Every year the Captain spent his winter cutting wood in the Adirondack Mountains, and in the early spring he and his brother, Dan, loaded the lumber onto their two barges and hauled it to New York City's busy harbor. There he would sell his lumber, pick up goods to fill their barges, and return west to Buffalo, where the Canal emptied into the Niagara River and then into the Great Lakes.

"Canawlers", those rugged families who traveled the Canal from early spring until the waters froze each winter, had stories that became legends through the years. This is the story of one of Captain John's family adventures as they hauled their goods from Rome to New York City's harbor on their first trip in the year of 1850. His daughter, Sarah, thirteen, and her cousin, Jack, fourteen, are part of his crew, along with Minnie the mule, and her sisters, Maude and Molly.

In this first book of Erie Canal adventures, Minnie and Sarah both dislike Mike, the family's "hogee" (the person who walks with the mule on the towpath that runs along the edge of the Canal). Mike is a surly man who is mean to the mules – and to Sarah and Jack. As they travel east to New York City a series of bank robberies seem to follow their path. Before long, Sarah and Minnie begin to suspect that Mike is working with the robber. All the way to Watervliet, where the mules and Mike are left while the family leaves the Canal to be pulled by a steam-powered tug down the Hudson River to New York City, the robberies continue.

In New York City, Sarah and her cousin, Jack spot Mike and a stranger (who Sarah insists fits the description of the robber). When they return to Watervliet to pick up the mules on their way home, Mike denies being in New York City.

Read how Sarah and Minnie prove their case, and solve the robberies!

Chapter ONE

The Adventure Begins

Come on – come on! Let's get started! Minnie pawed the ground restlessly and butted Sarah's blonde braids gently.

Sarah giggled as she stroked Minnie's gray muzzle. "I know you want to get going, Minnie, but Pa has to get everything on board first. See, he's just loading Molly."

Minnie turned her head to look at the big barge floating in the canal next to them. *Sarah is right.* She waited as the Captain prodded her sister up the plank from the towpath. *It seems like I have been standing here forever! Maude must already be down below in the bow-stable. Whoa! Here comes Jack! We must be ready to leave!* She nudged Sarah again, and twitched her long ears excitedly.

Sarah turned as her cousin, Jack, ran up and reached for the reins she was holding. She frowned. "I want to lead Minnie for a while. Papa promised I could this year."

"I know, but he wants me to start until we get out of the village." Jack grinned.

"Oh, all right, but I am going to walk with you." Sarah wrinkled her pert nose, making her freckles crinkle.

Minnie knew that Jack was older than Sarah, and liked to tease her. She liked both of them, but she knew how Sarah felt. Her sister, Molly, was a year older than her. *But I am starting out this year!* She snorted happily.

"Hey, you two! Let's get a move on!" Captain John

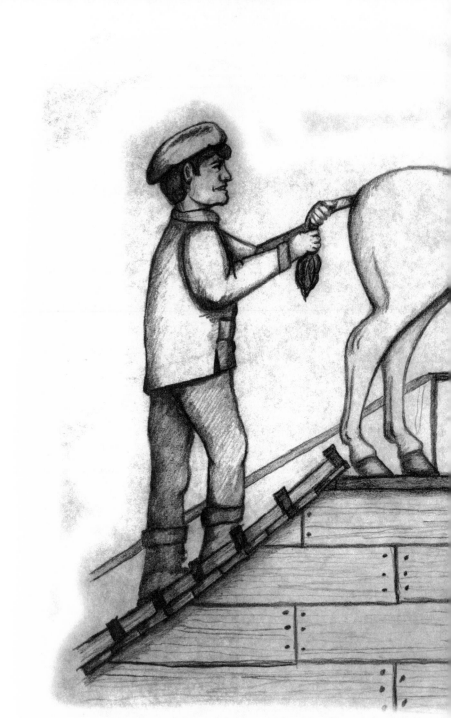

C'mon, C'mon let's get started!

Fairweather stowed the landing planks inside the boat and waved to them with a big grin on his tanned face. *Even his big black mustache looks happy!* Minnie took her first step down the towpath beside Jack. Sarah skipped, happily keeping pace with them.

"How far will we get today, do you think, Jack?"

Minnie leaned down so that she could hear his answer. She would like to know that too. She could feel the barge pulling against the long lines leading from her harness, back to the hooks that tied her to the boat. *I remember the first time that I saw that barge*, she mused as she stepped daintily along the gravel path. *I thought I would never be able to pull it, but look at me now!* Her ears twitched happily, and her long, tasseled tail swung back and forth with happy abandon. *No problem! But, I will probably be glad to hand this chore over to Maude or Molly by the end of my shift.*

She remembered last year when she and Molly took turns with their older sister, pulling the big boat. They had each walked for about six hours and then rested while the next mule took over. *I can't believe that Captain John gave me the first shift!* She snorted happily.

"Uncle John says he wants to make it through the lock near Utica before he beds down tonight." Jack looked up at the sun, where it rode high in the sky. "We got such a late start that it may be real late." He gave Sarah a lofty grin. "You will probably be asleep before that happens."

"I will not!" Sarah was indignant. "I am going to stay up until we tie up for the night."

Minnie was glad to hear that they were not going to travel all night. She knew some of the canal boatmen did that. *I sleep much better when we are not moving. When the water is rough it upsets my stomach.* She shook her head as she reflected happily that this summer promised to be a good trip.

The barge slipped smoothly through the rippling water of the canal as Captain John steered it from his seat at the back of the boat. His brother, Dan, chewed on his pipe and waved to a "canawler" coming the other way. Sarah's mother and Jack's mother were below in the galley storing all of their kitchen supplies away in the cupboards.

Minnie heard a noise at the front of the barge, and turned her head to see Mike, the extra hand who would walk one shift along the towpath with one of the mules. *I am glad he is not walking with me. I don't like him.* She snorted. The captain had brought him to the stable to look over the team, and Mike told him that Minnie looked too young to pull her weight all summer. *I would have kicked him if he had been close enough!*

"Ho, the canal! Good Luck! Wish I was going with you!" The voice came from the open window of one of the factories they were passing on Martin Street, close to the railroad tracks. The banks of the canal were lined with steel and copper mills, and the workers waved from the windows that were opened to catch the afternoon breeze.

Sarah reached up to pat Minnie excitedly. "We are really on our way! I can hardly believe it!"

Chapter TWO

Ghosts Out Tonight

It is really dark! Minnie tried not to feel nervous, but the long shadows along the edges of the towpath made her glad her shift would soon be over.

Sarah was riding on her broad back. Jack had boosted her up there a while ago when her tired legs refused to keep up with Jack's long steps. They had been walking for over five hours.

"Hey, Sarah, right along here is where I saw the ghost last year!" Jack looked up at his cousin with a mischievous grin.

"You did not! There is no such thing as a ghost, and you know it!" Sarah was suddenly wide awake. In spite of her brave words, she looked closely at the tall black bushes they were passing. The lantern on the front of the barge did not throw its light very far ahead, and the path grew dark only a few feet in front of them. Minnie turned her head to look too.

"Yes, I did…Remember, I told you about it? There is a big old haunted house just down the line here, next to the graveyard." Jack pointed ahead as the towpath curved around a bend in the canal. "See? There is the cemetery."

Sarah and Minnie drew shaky breaths as they followed his finger to where he was pointing. The moon was almost full and its light shone eerily on a small cemetery with skinny old stones leaning crookedly in the soil around them. A picket fence closed in the headstones and a sudden draft of

Ghosts out tonight?

wind made the old gate creak. Sarah jumped and Minnie stopped, pulling back on Jack's hold on her reins.

"Come on, Minnie," he coaxed. "I won't let the ghost get you. Besides, I heard ghosts only like girls." Before Sarah could answer him, a big house came into view. It rose tall and dark, with windows reflecting the moon's light in a ghostly shimmer. She shivered, and Minnie knew just how she felt! Goose-bumps covered her gray hide.

"Oh – it is only an old abandoned house." Sarah's voice trembled a little, but she tried to sound scornful.

"No way. I am telling you, lots of canawlers will tell you that they have seen ghosts moving around in there." Jack nodded sagely. "Last year I am sure I saw one myself."

"Well, I am glad to say that I don't see any in there today." Sarah laughed.

Oh, what is that? Minnie stepped ahead and her foot touched something wet and slimy. She jerked Jack's arm again as she planted her feet firmly and refused to move ahead.

"Come on, Minnie. What is the matter? Don't tell me that you are afraid of ghosts too?" Jack laughed and took a step ahead, pulling on her reins. His foot hit a slippery spot and he crashed, falling flat on his hands and knees. His hands landed in a cold, slimy puddle and he gave a scared "Oof!"

"What is it? Are you okay?" Sarah slid down from Minnie's back, forgetting her own fright as she saw Jack fall. Her long brown skirt swished as she rushed to his side. Minnie watched as she bent over her cousin and reached into her skirt pocket to take out a candle. She lit the taper, and gave a shaky little laugh. "It is only a big old branch, silly. See?" She held her candle up and Minnie gave a snort of relief. One of the trees along the towpath had lost a big leafy branch, and it had dropped down across their path.

"Oh…yeah, I see." Jack got slowly to his feet and handed Minnie's reins to Sarah. "Here, you hold Minnie and I will move it out of the way." His voice was sheepish.

"What is going on down there? Why aren't we moving?" Captain John called to them. Turning her head, Minnie could see Captain Dan peering over the rails of the barge where it floated just behind them.

"Uh – just a branch on the path." Jack called back. "I will move it in just a minute."

"We will be down to help." His father called. Captain John steered the barge to the side of the canal. In just a short time the two men were beside them, and it took only a few minutes to drag the big branch away from the towpath.

"I am glad to see you didn't panic." Captain John smiled at them. "If you had not kept a level head someone could have gone into the canal."

"Or been caught by the ghost that lives in the haunted house." Sarah laughed, fully recovered now from her scare.

Her father chuckled. "Jack's been telling ghost stories again, has he?" He looked at the old house behind them. "Some day I will have to tell you some of the tales I heard as a boy when my father sailed this canal." He laughed. "As long as we have stopped, I think it is time to change shifts. Sarah, run back to the barge and tell Mike to get Maude out of the bow stable while I unharness Minnie."

He reached up to pat Minnie and gave her a good scratch behind her ears where she liked to be rubbed. "Good job, Girl. You have earned a good feed and a chance to rest."

I could not agree more, Captain. Minnie brayed.

Chapter THREE

Into the Lock

What is that? Minnie opened a sleepy eye. Next to her, Molly brayed and backed nervously away from her manger.

"Get back there!" Mike snarled, yanking Molly's reins and slapping her viciously on the nose.

You stop that! Minnie reached over and snapped her teeth only an inch away from his shoulder.

Mike turned and slapped her with the strap he held in his hand, and Minnie reared, edging away from him.

"Hey!" Jack came bounding down the cleated ramp from the deck to the stable, with Sarah close behind him. "Don't slap the mules! My uncle doesn't believe in that!"

"No, he doesn't, and I am going to tell!" Sarah whirled around and scrambled up the ramp before Mike could stop her.

"These dang mules are so dumb that I have to get their attention before I move them," Mike said angrily.

"Not that way." Captain Fairweather came down the ramp with Sarah, and his voice was firm. "I won't tolerate anyone hitting my animals. You had best keep that in mind." His face was stern. "Come on, Molly, that's a good girl." He took her reins from Mike and led her up the incline to the deck.

"I will remember that you tattler." Mike snarled at Sarah as he passed her.

"Don't you worry, Minnie. I won't let him be mean to you." Sarah stuck her tongue out at him as he disappeared up on deck. She stroked Minnie's soft gray coat and started brushing her. "I wish Pa had never hired that man."

Me too. We are going to have trouble with him. Minnie relaxed under Sarah's long strokes.

Over in the end stall Maude nodded and twitched her ears in agreement. *Mike is one mean man!*

Before long Jack came back and helped Sarah open the wooden blinds that covered the front of the bow-stable windows and fastened them up to the low ceiling.

That's better! Minnie stuck her head out through the opening and felt the cool morning breeze blowing the smell of the stable away.

"Look! We are coming to a lock!" Sarah crowded next to Minnie at the window, and Minnie obligingly inched over to give her more room.

Jack ran back to the deck. He would help untie Molly's lines from the barge when they reached the gates. Mike would lead her up the sloping path and over to the other side of the lock where they would wait for the barge to come through to the other side.

"I fell asleep before we went through the lock last night. This is the first one for me this year." Sarah reached over to fondle Minnie's soft muzzle excitedly. "I can't wait!"

Minnie was nervous. Usually she seemed to be the mule who waited on the towpath. This would be her first time inside the lock this year. She moved restlessly as the big wooden gates loomed before them.

"Don't be scared, I am right here with you," Sarah comforted her.

Together they watched the two men on the platform before them swing the long paddles that opened the gates so they could float slowly inside. "It looks like a big box! And we are right near the top of it." Sarah craned her neck to see the top of the lock's sides.

This is not so bad – Oooh, no! We are falling! Minnie snorted. Her stomach lurched as the floor seemed to sink beneath her. She pawed the straw beneath her feet and brayed.

"Don't worry, Minnie. We are just being lowered to the next level in the canal." Sarah tried to sound brave. "Remember, Jack says we get lowered at every lock until we get to Albany. It has something to do with the sea level. Mama says I will probably learn all about it this summer."

Suddenly, the barge seemed to steady itself and that sinking sensation went away. Minnie drew a deep breath of relief. Looking out the window again, she saw nothing but dark stones on either side of her. Startled again, she stretched her head out the window and looked up. The walls were high above them! They were in the bottom of the lock.

"There! The other gates are opening and we will be moving out into the canal again." Sarah leaned out the window to see better.

Ooh, here we go again! I don't like this! The barge suddenly moved ahead quickly and water rippled all around them.

"Pa says we get "swelled" out of the locks. No one is pulling us so the man at the gate makes water push us out." Sarah explained when she saw Minnie move nervously.

Is that right? Minnie relaxed as they moved out into the canal. She could see Molly standing on the towpath with Mike yanking on her reins.

"That was fun!" Sarah hugged Minnie's neck. She laughed. "You will see, before we get to Albany, you won't mind the locks at all."

Maybe yes, maybe no. My stomach is still shaking! I think I like being the mule on the towpath. Minnie twitched her ears and munched her oats.

Chapter FOUR

There is Money in the Air

It was early afternoon when Captain Fairweather's barge docked at the Herkimer Marina. Jack and Sarah came running down to the bow-stable to lead Minnie up the cleated ramp to the deck. Captain John stood waiting for them at the rail.

"You take her reins, Jack, and I will take her tail."

Minnie had been through this before, but she was always shaky. She stepped up onto the slanting plank that went from the top of the rail to the towpath below them. In spite of the cleats in the plank, it was a steep walk to the ground.

Be careful! Hold on tight! I don't want to fall off this board! Minnie tossed her head nervously as Jack led her down the ramp. She felt Captain John pull back on her tail to help slow her progress, and she whinnied in relief when she set foot on the gravel of the towpath.

Molly stood with Mike holding her reins, waiting to climb the ramp. She backed as far away from him as she could. *You are lucky you do not have to walk with this one! He is as nasty as he can be.* She whinnied at her sister as Minnie went past.

I agree! Oh, oh, maybe I spoke too soon. Minnie turned her head as the captain spoke to Mike.

"The family is going to make a quick trip into town. We need to pick up some supplies. As soon as you have settled

There is money in the air.

Molly below come back and hold onto Minnie until we get back. Give her a good feed while you are here."

Surprisingly, Mike did not object. "I will be right back. You don't expect me to do any more walking this afternoon I hope. I need to catch some sleep when we leave."

"Jack and Sarah will walk when we leave here. Just stay with Minnie until we return. It should not take us too long." The captain stood patiently while Mike went up the ramp with Molly. He grinned as he watched Jack try his hand at prodding her from behind.

He and his wife and Sarah stood with his brother and Jack's mother until Jack came running and nimbly jumped off the ramp.

"Mike is on his way. I think he got himself a drink to have while we are gone." Jack scowled. "He is certainly not very friendly. Is he going all the way to New York with us?"

"Probably. We need the extra man on such a long haul. Otherwise someone would have to walk a double shift every day. As it is, your dad picks up the third shift every day."

Mike came down the ramp with Minnie's feedbag over his shoulder. He carried a mug of dark liquor in his hand that sloshed as he jumped to the path. He quickly lifted it and drained it all in one long swallow, wiping his whiskers with the back of his hand.

Captain Fairweather handed him Minnie's reins. "No more drinking when you handle the mules, Mike. Give her a feed and stay with her while we are gone."

Mike hung his mug on his belt and slid the straps of the feedbag over Minnie's head as she rolled her eyes at him. "Mind your manners or you will wish you had." He gave her a rough slap on her shoulder.

You are lucky that I have this bag over my mouth! I would love to give you a good nip! Minnie shook her head indignantly before she settled down to eat her oats. As she munched contentedly a few minutes later, she heard a noise just ahead of them. The tall bushes that lined the banks beside the dirt road parted, and a big man stepped onto the towpath. He looked around quickly and grinned as he spied Mike.

"There you are! Right on time! Here, be quick. I don't want to be seen down here." He took a canvas bag from his duffel and shoved it at Mike.

What is going on? Minnie wondered. The man had a red beard and a drooping mustache. He wore a long black coat and a wide-brimmed black hat. He smelled of sweat. *He smells worse than the stable when it needs cleaning!* She tried to back away from him and Mike.

"Hold on there!" Mike yanked her back. "How much did you get?" He turned back to the other man.

"Enough. You will see when you get your share when we meet at Amsterdam. Make sure you get that hidden until then, and don't try any of your tricks with me."

"I'm your brother – would I do that? Anyhow, where would I go? I want the rest of my share. I'll see you there." Mike reached up and yanked Minnie's feedbag roughly from her head.

Hey! I am not finished. Minnie brayed her displeasure.

"Shut up!" Mike gave her a slap on the muzzle, wrapping her reins around his wrist as he took the canvas sack and stuffed it down into her bag before he slung it over his shoulder.

"Okay. I am on my way. See you in two days." The stranger melted quickly back into the bushes as Minnie heard voices. Someone was coming down the road towards them.

It was Sarah and Jack, running ahead of their parents. "Minnie! Look what we got for you!" She held out a big straw hat with a wide brim. "Now the sun won't get into your eyes."

Minnie whinnied her approval. *That's nice…but what about my ears? They won't fit under that, will they?*

Sarah had thought of that. "Papa is going to cut holes for your ears before we start again. He got a hat for Molly and Maude too."

"Yeah. Sarah thought her sunbonnet wouldn't fit you." Jack grinned as he watched Sarah try to put the hat on Minnie's head.

"Just a minute. Let me cut some holes." Her father took the hat and pulled out his pocket knife. "There!" He sat the hat at a jaunty angle atop Minnie's head, with her long ears poking out just in back of the wide brim.

Now I won't have to squint in the sun. Minnie pawed the ground and brayed her approval. She was so pleased that she forgot all about Mike and the man who had passed him the canvas bag. In just a few minutes the captain and his family were back on board with the rest of their packages stowed in their cabin. Mike had disappeared below deck.

"Okay, you two can help us make some time." The captain smiled at Sarah and Jack, as he settled into his chair with the tiller that steered the barge comfortably in his hands. His brother finished stocking the water barrels and food bins lined up just in front of the family cabin.

"I wish we had been in Herkimer when the bank was robbed this morning, don't you, Jack?" Sarah skipped along beside him as they started down the towpath.

"That would have been something! The police told Pa that the robber took the factory payroll that was delivered last night. He got a lot of money."

"Did you hear him say that this was the second robbery this week? He said the Utica bank was robbed yesterday. It must have happened after we went through the lock." Sarah looked thoughtful as she stroked Minnie's neck.

A bank robbery? Money? Minnie thought about that man who had given Mike a canvas bag. *Could he be a robber? Why would he give Mike money? I remember what he said*

about getting a lot of something. She shook her head, watching the shadow her new hat made on the towpath. *I guess I had better think about that later. Right now I am going to pay attention to where I am walking. I don't want to fall in the canal.*

Chapter FIVE

Score One for Minnie

Minnie walked carefully up the ramp from the towpath late that afternoon. Jack stood at the rail, ready to lead her down the long ramp into the bow stable as Sarah gently pushed on her rear quarters to stop her from slipping back.

As always, Minnie thought, *This is not my favorite thing to do. I will be glad to get into my stable safely. There! Home again.* She drew a long breath of relief and watched Captain Fairweather back her sister out of her stall.

See you later, girls. Behave yourselves. Maude whinnied as she took her turn climbing the long ramp to the deck. Captain Dan would walk with her as they moved towards the city of Fonda where another lock awaited them.

Where is Mike? I hope he sleeps until he has to walk again. He didn't let me finish my meal. I am hungry! Minnie looked over at Molly as their sister left the stable.

No such luck! He is coming out of his room right now. Molly turned her head to look back as Mike stumbled out of his room that was just a few feet behind them.

He paid no attention to them as he went to the hooks where the feedbags hung and reached into the one Minnie had used. He looked around nervously as he pulled the canvas bag out, and walked over to the big locker where he kept his clothes. It was directly in back of Molly's stall. Minnie watched as he stuffed the bag down under the contents

Score one for Minnie!

already there. He slammed the door, and stood up, lurching unsteadily into Molly. She brayed loudly in alarm, and he grabbed a leather strap off the wall to strike her viciously across her rump.

You stop that! Minnie brayed as she struck out with her hind hoof and caught him on the seat of his pants.

He swung around and angrily used the strap on Minnie as Sarah came running down the ramp.

"I am going to tell my father! He told you not to hit the mules!" Sarah's eyes sparked with anger.

"You keep your trap shut!" Mike reached out to grab her, but she was too quick for him. She spun around and bounded up the ramp.

Mike quickly hung the strap back on the wall before the captain came down with his daughter.

"What is going on? Sarah said you just hit Minnie." He faced Mike with his hands on his hips, and his blue eyes were just as angry as Sarah's.

"She kicked me! What was I supposed to do? Just stand there and take it?" Mike was defiant.

"You must have done something to her or she would not do that." Sarah glared at him.

Good for you! Tell the captain to fire him. He is a bad man. Minnie snorted, and Molly nervously pawed the straw in her stall. She was scared of Mike.

"I have warned you repeatedly, Mike. If you continue to abuse these animals, I will drop you at the next port." Captain Fairweather's voice was quiet, but he meant what he said.

"Okay! But this kid of yours is nothing but a trouble-maker. Tell her to stay out of my way." Mike's voice was surly.

"Give Minnie and Molly a good feed, Sarah." Her father ignored Mike's surly manner. He turned and went back up the ramp to continue on their way down the canal.

Sarah dipped a pail of oats and dumped it into Minnie's

feed-bin. She patted her on the nose as she moved back to get Molly's food. "Don't you girls worry. Pa won't let Mike hurt you." She comforted them.

Mike stood at the open door of his room and watched her. He took a drink from the bottle on a table just inside his room. "You are nothing but trouble, Missy. I am going to take care of you and that mule before I am done."

Minnie felt a shiver of fear race down her spine. *He scares me. He really hates Sarah and me.* She watched him until he turned and went back into his room.

Up on deck, Sarah carried a basket of vegetables her mother had just asked her to peel for their evening meal, and sat down on a stool next to her father. She loved the smell of his pipe, and he always told her stories about the places they passed on the canal. "Jack says it is supposed to be so hot in New York City that rich people who can afford it, leave the city every summer and don't go back until sometime in September. Is that true?"

He nodded. "It is a little early in the season yet, but I think we will meet some of the packet boats as we near Albany. Where is your mother?"

"She is baking an apple pie for supper." Sarah started snapping the crisp green beans they had purchased in Herkimer. "Pa, Jack says that General Herkimer, you know the man who the village is named after, haunts that cemetery we went by near Oriskany. That is just a story – isn't it?"

Her father grinned. "There is such a story. It is told by some old timers, but I have yet to see his ghost. Some of the area around Schoharie Creek near there was called Palatine Bridge by the old time canawlers. Did Jack tell you about the Palatine Bridge Fairies?"

"Fairies? You are telling me another story – right?" She smiled as she looked up at him.

"Well – tales are part fact, and part fiction, I guess.

Canawlers who have sailed the canal for years will tell you that the Palatine Fairies have helped them find game when they needed food. They would appear and point out game, and when the hungry hunters tried to thank them, they would disappear."

"What did they look like? Did they have little wings on their shoulders, and long swishy dresses?" Sarah laughed.

Her father chuckled. "I never saw one of them myself, so I don't know." He took one of the beans from her basket and chewed it thoughtfully. "As far as General Herkimer goes, he did lose his leg in the battle of Oriskany, when he and his men were battling to save Fort Stanwix in Rome from the Iroquois Indians and the English soldiers who tried to take it from them after our country declared our independence back in 1776." He winked at her. "So, who knows, maybe he has stayed to haunt the place where he was wounded."

"The English people didn't like us?" Sarah was surprised. "But – we are part English, aren't we?"

"Yes." Her father agreed. "My ancestors came over from England. Your mother's family immigrated from Ireland. A lot of her family helped to build this canal. Those early years were hard. Everyone who came over to this country knew that this part of New York was important land to own. The waterway from New York City, west to what we call Buffalo now, and beyond to the Great Lakes, was hard fought for. Water travel was the best way to head west, and this was the most direct route."

"But you just said the English people didn't like us." Sarah frowned.

"You have to understand that the only native Americans are really the Indians. They were here when explorers landed in the United States. While everyone was trying to claim land for their own countries, they fought among themselves. The Iroquois Indians who lived in this state became friendly with English settlers. When some settlers decided they wanted to be independent and form their own country, the Iroquois Indians sided with the English who were still loyal to the Crown. Some of the Indians, the Algonquins, and other members of the Oneida Nation of Indians, were friendly with the French settlers who were loyal to France. They fought with them. You are studying that in school. Isn't that right?"

"We have studied that a little," she admitted. "But I have never really understood it. I just thought everyone in this country is American. I never thought about us coming from a lot of different places."

Her father laughed again. "There are more different nationalities here than in any other country, I think. Remember, while our ancestors are Irish and English, many of the settlers who came to live in the village that is now Frankfort came from Germany. Frankfort was once known as German Flats. Did you know that?"

Sarah nodded. "Yes. My teacher read about that when we read about the battle of Fort Stanwix in Rome when they flew our flag for the first time. General Herkimer marched from Herkimer to German Flats to help."

"Exactly." He ran his fingers through his dark hair. "We are a mixed lot."

Chapter SIX

Going East

"Another lock coming up!" Captain Fairweather called. Sarah came out of the cabin where she had been helping her mother and ran to the bow of the barge. Her mother followed, wiping her hands on her big apron. They watched the gate's attendants swing the steering paddles to open the doors for them.

"When we come out of this lock, look up on the cliff, and you will see something that will surprise you."

"What? What will I see?" Sarah asked eagerly.

"Just wait." Her mother smiled at her.

The fat man spinning the door paddle spat as they passed him, and a stream of dark tobacco juice hit the water.

"Ugh! I am glad Papa doesn't chew tobacco!" Sarah wrinkled her nose.

The gates swung closed behind them, and once more she saw that they were near the top of the walls of the lock. This time she was more prepared for that sinking sensation as the water started to lower their boat. She could see Mike walking Molly along the towpath to the other side of the lock, and she saw that Jack had jumped ashore while his father's boat was separated from theirs going through the lock. It was not too long before the gates at the far end of the lock opened and they were "swelled" out into the canal again.

"Over there, Sarah." Abigail Fairchild pointed to the stone cliff ahead.

"It is a man's face! Who is it? Who carved it there?" Sarah looked in awe at what appeared to be the profile of a man in the face of the cliff.

Her mother laughed. "It is not a carving. Over the years the water and the blasting that has been done here to make a passage has made that rock look like a man's face. No one did it on purpose, but it is a big attraction for the tourists that come past it."

"We haven't seen any tourist boats since we left Rome. I was hoping that we would." Sarah remembered the stories that Jack had told her about the Packet Boats full of wealthy people who took the ride up the canal from New York City. He said they went to some of the big resort hotels along the canal. "Pa said Oneida Lake is one of the places that they stop – at Sylvan Beach. We have been there. Remember when Jack and I went on the rides next to the canal?"

Abigail nodded. We couldn't afford to stay at the hotels there. Some of the tourists go all the way to Syracuse and Rochester, or even to Buffalo. And some leave the canal farther west and go by carriage up into the Adirondack Mountains. They have beautiful hotels up there."

Sarah thought her mother sounded wistful. *I'll bet Mama would like to stay in one of those places – but I like staying on our barge.*

She walked with Jack again that afternoon along the towpath. Mike was eating an early dinner before going to rest on his bunk.

"What are we having for supper? I thought I smelled apple pie. It sure smelled good." Jack rubbed his stomach. "I'm hungry already."

"We are having roast beef and mashed potatoes – and Mama baked apple pie for dessert." She grinned. "If Mike doesn't eat all of it."

"He had better not! Walking makes me hungry."

"I brought you some cookies your Ma baked." She reached into the deep pocket of her dress, and handed him a molasses cookie. Aunt Mabel says you are a bottomless pit when it comes to food." She teased him.

"Ahoy the barge!" Sarah looked out at a barge just coming even with theirs from the other direction, going West. She saw her father go to the rail to greet the burly man who had hailed him as their boats drifted close together.

"I wonder who that is? He must know Papa." Sara watched the two men reach out to shake hands.

"That is Captain O'Malley. I met him last summer." Jack laughed. "He is quite a character. Oh, I think we are going to stop to visit with him." He saw his uncle steer the barge to the edge of the canal.

When the landing plank was lowered, Sarah ran back to join her father aft on the deck, just as her father asked the big man where he was heading.

"Syracuse first, to unload, then on to Buffalo with a load of salt." He looked down at Sarah as she ran up to the rail, and his black beard split in a wide smile. "And who is this mite? He was dressed in a flannel shirt and overalls, and a cap with a long visor rode the top of his bushy dark hair. He was the biggest man she had ever seen.

"This is my daughter, Sarah." Her father put his arm around her shoulders. "Sarah this is Captain Christopher O'Malley." He looked down at her. "I have known the Captain since I was a boy no older than you are now. He and my father shipped together sometimes."

The captain engulfed her small hands in his huge ones. "She don't favor you, John – thank the good Lord." He laughed heartily, enjoying his own humor.

"No. She looks like her mother." Her father was not

28

offended. "Go and get your mother." He turned back to the Captain. "Can you spare the time for a visit? We are just changing mules, and we are about ready to eat. Can you join us? Dan and his family are with us."

"Your brother is here too? Good – I can always take time to eat. Just let me tell Sal she don't have to feed me."

Sarah and her mother came close and she heard her father say, "Sal? You married since I saw you last?"

The Captain roared with laughter. "No – Sal is my cook – and First Mate. Picked her up in Troy and she is goin' the distance with me."

"Oh." Sarah thought her father hesitated. "Uh – would she like to join us for supper? We have plenty. Don't we?" He looked down at his wife as she came to stand next to him.

"Of course we do! It is good to see you Chris. It has been a long time."

"Too long!" The Captain's burly arms spanned the distance to hug her.

"We have plenty of food. Ask your…"

"Cook, Abigail. The Captain's not married." Her father said hastily.

"Your cook, she finished smoothly, "to join us too." She turned to Sarah. "Go and tell Aunt Mabel supper will be ready in just a few minutes, and tell her that we have company, in case she has not seen the Captain." She turned back to him. "Our families eat together, and it gives us a chance to visit."

She came back a few minutes later with a basket of fresh rolls Aunt Mabel gave her to carry, and her eyes nearly popped when she saw the woman Mama was talking to. She had bright yellow hair, and her eyes were outlined with so much black kohl that they looked like two purple grapes. Aunt Mabel poked her to make her move from where she had stopped dead at the top of the landing plank. The lady wore a shiny red dress, covered with a grimy white apron tied around her ample waist. *I've never seen a cook that looked like this lady.*

She turned as Sarah and her aunt approached and smiled at her. Sarah was fascinated by a tiny black mole fastened at the corner of her red lips, that seemed to go up and down as she talked. "This must be your daughter, Abigail. She looks like you."

Her mother nodded. "This is my sister-in-law, Mabel, Sal."

As they turned to go down the short flight of steps to the galley, Sal followed, looking pleased. "You don't know how good it is to have females to talk with! I get mighty tired of those hogees that the Cap'n brings aboard." She smiled at all of them impartially, and Sarah found herself liking her.

Before long they were gathered around the table, and Sarah and Jack listened while the grownups recalled old times. Sal ate hugely, and praised every bite she took, making Abigail and Mabel flush with pleasure. In spite of all the makeup she wore, and her strange clothes, Sarah decided she liked Sal very much.

Aunt Mabel asked her how she happened to get the job cooking on the Captain's boat, and she looked down at her plate, biting her lip.

"I found Sal without a job in Troy," he answered for her. "She was having a hard time making it, and I needed a cook. She needed a job just as bad, so I asked her along for the trip, and it has worked out good." Captain O'Malley continued jovially, "Sal steers as good as any man while I be the hogee, and I was able to get rid of the extra man. Never had me a daughter, and Sal and I get along just fine."

"You are hauling by yourselves?" Sarah's uncle looked surprised.

"Old Sam Stinger is still with me. He is tending to the mules while we are eating."

"I'll fix him a plate." Abigail promised.

"That is mighty nice of you." His weathered face split in another grin. "Say – we ran into some excitement in Amsterdam this morning! They had a big bank robbery – and the thief got away with close to ten thousand dollars from the gristmill's payroll!"

"There was a bank robbery in Utica and one in Herkimer as we were locking through. Did you hear a description of the thief that held up the bank in Amsterdam?" Captain John lit his pipe, as he sat back in his chair.

"Yep. Big fellow, with a red beard." Sal said she was glad I was aboard. She figured all men with a beard look alike somehow." He laughed heartily.

"Maybe he's on his way to New York City, just like us." Sarah whispered to Jack.

"Sure looks like it, don't it?" He whispered back. "We will be in Amsterdam tomorrow. Maybe they will catch him before we get there."

Chapter SEVEN

Passing Amsterdam

"We are close to Amsterdam. When we reach this point, we are in Dutch country." Captain John pointed to the rich green fields they were passing. "Now you will see some big cities, bigger than any you have ever visited."

"Are we going to stop in Amsterdam?" *I want to hear more about the robbery there that Captain O'Malley told us about.*

"No. Maybe on our way back. We will only stop to lock through when we have to. I want to get as close to Schenectady as we can today. Cohoes is just a short way from there, and I want to get that stretch behind us as fast as we can."

"Why? What is so special about Cohoes?" She was disappointed that they were not going ashore in Amsterdam. Already, she could see the factories along the shoreline, and the smoke from their stacks rose lazily in the distance. "Mama said that Amsterdam was where you bought the pearl buttons you brought back last year. She says they make them there. Those buttons look so pretty on the dress that Mama made me last winter. I love the way they have different colors in them."

"Cohoes starts the sixteen locks that we will be going through. They are all within about three-and-a-half miles. We will be dropping close to two-hundred feet in sea level down that stretch, and it takes us almost a whole day to get through all of them, with good luck."

"Really?" Sarah was impressed. She had grown accustomed to "locking through" as they had floated down the canal, but every lock was different. Some of the gatekeepers were nice, and some of them were mean. There were gatekeepers that seemed to think only about the quarter they collected from them for their service.

Her father tamped the tobacco down in his pipe with his thumb. It was early afternoon, and Sarah was peeling potatoes for their next meal as she sat next to him. Her mother was hanging clothes on the line between the cabin and the bow-stable. "Once we lock through at Cohoes, it won't be long before we pasture the mules and join the tow down the Hudson River. Before we reach Albany though, we have to go through twenty-seven locks – all within a fifteen mile stretch."

"When will we get to Albany, Pa? Tomorrow?" Sarah was excited at the thought of the journey down the Hudson River. Her father had told her stories about what it was like last winter.

"From Amsterdam, we pass Cranesville, Rotterdam and Scotia before we come to Schenectady and go around it. We might tie up there for a night." Her father stretched to ease his tired muscles.

"But when will we get to Albany?" Sarah persisted.

"Maybe the day after tomorrow, if we do not run into any bad weather." He pointed to a barge coming towards them. "Here comes your first Tourist Packet Boat for the season."

It was late afternoon now, and she heard music floating across the water as the sleek white boat drew closer. She ran to the rail and watched people who were lined up along the high rails of the other boat. Her mother came to the rail to watch with her. There were people sitting on chairs on the roof of the long cabin that ran the length of the middle of the boat. Men, wearing striped dress jackets and straw hats, leaned casually against the boat's supports. Their light-colored pants contrasted with the bright colors of the gowns the women standing next to them wore. Sarah stared at the beautiful dresses and elaborate hats. Some of the women held parasols to protect them from the sun. As she waved to them, some of them waved back.

The Packet Boat was as long as the *Fairchild I* and its enclosed cabin was much longer than theirs. The space her father used for hauling freight was devoted to making the passengers comfortable.

"Where do they sleep, Mama? Are there cuddy's for their beds inside that cabin, like in ours?"

Abigail smiled. "That is a good question. Your father says that is a big problem. There is not enough space for individual bedrooms if they haul enough people to make money for the boat's owners. Some of the owners hang hammocks, and they can be pretty tricky to get into. Some of them spread mattresses out on the floor of the cabin after meals are served. It must get pretty hot in there later in the summer."

"You mean that everyone sleeps in one room? The men and women?" Sarah was shocked.

Her mother laughed. "I would guess that they hang curtains between the men and the women's quarters. I really don't know though."

"If many of those men snore like Pa does sometimes, it certainly must get pretty noisy." Sarah chuckled.

Her mother looked thoughtful as they watched the boat proceed down the canal. "I don't know how much longer the Packet Boats will keep operating. Now that the trains are running from the city to the Adirondacks, a lot of people are going that way. I thing the fact that they get so filthy from the coal dust that drives the trains, makes packet boating the better way to travel. But the trains keep improving, and they may take business away from water travel."

"I noticed that the railroad tracks seem to run right along a lot of the same paths that the canal follows." Sarah frowned. "The trains sure make an awful racket when they get close to us. Sometimes it scares the mules."

"Yes. That is true. Your papa is a little worried about the trains taking some of his freight business." Her mother sighed.

"You mean that we wouldn't tow down the canal anymore?" Sarah was dismayed.

"That won't happen for a long time. Don't worry about it." Her mother started back towards the cabin. "Let's get set up for supper."

They tied up that night just a mile from Schenectady. "Tomorrow we will be spending the day going through the locks that take us past Cohoes. Abigail, I may be needing your help at the wheel." The Captain yawned wearily.

"Why? What is going to happen, Papa?" Sarah was puzzled.

"Probably nothing. It is just that the Cohoes Falls are pretty tough. When we reach Crescent, just a short ways from there we pass across an aqueduct that takes us across the Mohawk River and around the falls to Cohoes. You will see all the mills along the shore, because the water gives them the power to run their machinery. The woolens and the cotton for your dresses are manufactured there."

"Your father lost one of his friends in an accident while he was locking through here a few years ago," Mama said quietly. "He is always glad to put this stretch behind him."

Sarah went to bed in the little nook that the canawler called their "cuddy", and she was eager for the next day to come.

Chapter EIGHT

Another Bank Robbery!

Sarah jumped ashore before they entered each of the sixteen locks, and watched her uncle's boat follow them through. At each lock her father seemed to meet someone he had met before on the canal. There was so much canal traffic that they had to wait their turn in several of the locks.

By late afternoon she was becoming bewildered by all of the new people they had seen that day. She and Jack stood with a man named Max at the last lock they would have to go through today. He was a short, wiry little man who fascinated her as he accurately spit a stream of tobacco juice into a black metal spittoon about five feet away from him on the dock. Her father had pointed him out as they came to the lock, and when she went ashore, he introduced himself to her and Jack.

"I know both of your Pas." He wiped his chin on the back of his gnarled hand. "I been a canawler for many a year, but I never heard of the shenanigans we are seein' this year."

"What are shen…shenana…?" She faltered, not remembering the rest of the word.

"What goings on." He explained with a gap-toothed grin. "Ain't you heard about the bank robberies?"

"We have been hearing about robberies back along the canal in the cities we passed." Jack nodded. "You had robberies down this way too?"

"You bet! I heard we had a big one in Schenectady just this morning!" He shook his head. "And the po-lice tells me the thief got clean away again. I hear there has been at least six robberies in the past two weeks, and no one comes close to catching anyone!" His voice was almost admiring as he admitted how clever this thief was.

"I will bet it is the same man who robbed the banks in Utica and Herkimer when we went through there," Sarah said excitedly. "Did you hear what the robber looked like?"

"Yep. The bank manager said it was a big red-headed fellow with a beard. He got in before the bank opened and the manager was alone."

"The robbery in Schenectady – when did that happen? Mike went ashore there when we went through the lock, and he didn't mention hearing about it."

"Real early in the morning. Got in before the bank opened and made off with a bundle of money."

"Let's ask Mike if he heard about it." Sarah quivered with excitement. Jack nodded eagerly, and they ran back to the towpath where Mike was standing with the mules.

"Mike! Did you hear about a robbery back in Schenectady this morning when you went into town?" Sarah was breathless as she skidded to a stop beside him.

He frowned and yanked Minnie's bridle and bit viciously. "Yeah – I did hear something about a robbery. Didn't pay too much attention to it. Your Pa was waitin' on me to get started again." He yanked Minnie's halter again, so hard that her feed bag tipped. She backed away from him, braying loudly.

"We were just talking to that man." Sarah pointed back to where Max stood talking now to her father. "His name is Max and he knows Papa. He says there has been six bank robberies, and he had never heard of such shenanigans!" She was thrilled with the new word she had just learned. "That means goings-on." She explained loftily.

Mike didn't seem too interested. He yanked Minnie's feed bag off completely, and the mule reached over, nipping at him. He slapped at her muzzle and she pulled her head back from his range, rolling her eyes and stamping her feet.

Sarah tried not to giggle. *Minnie really does not like him – and I don't blame her.*

"It seems like they are going to New York City – just like us." Jack looked thoughtful. He wanted to tell Mike to stop being so rough with the mules, but he didn't quite dare.

Sarah felt a chill go down her spine. "Do you think the robber is really going to New York City too? "

"No. I don't!" Mike snarled "New York's a far piece from here. Most likely these robberies are being made by different men." He yanked the feed bags off from the other two feeding mules. "You two had better get on board. Looks like we are ready to move."

"He never pays any attention to what we tell him." Sarah complained as she led Minnie towards the loading plank.

"I don't like him. I am going to tell Pa how rough he is with the animals." Jack's face was grim as they started up the ramp.

Chapter NINE

Mike and Sarah Clash

"Sarah, first thing tomorrow I want you to get Mike's laundry for me from his room. I am going to try and wash one more time before we leave the canal. We start running in salt water as we go east, and I won't use it for washing clothes unless I have to." Her mother stirred the pot of chicken soup she had made that day when she was not helping Captain John at the wheel. "I am too tired to even think about doing laundry tonight."

Remembering what her mother said the next morning, Sarah went directly to Mike's room after doing her chores in the bow-stable. She knocked at the door. When Mike didn't answer, she timidly went in. ***He must be helping Pa.***

She wrinkled her nose at the way his room smelled of sweat and dirty clothes. His bed was unmade, and his discarded clothes were laying in heaps on the floor, and on the foot of his bunk.

"What do you think you are doing!" Mike's voice boomed behind her.

She had squatted beside his bunk to pick up some of his dirty socks, and she jumped at the sound of his voice. Looking up at him, she could see that he was furious. She felt herself start to tremble, but she faced him bravely. "Mama asked me to get your laundry so she could do it before we get to where we leave the mules." She was disgusted with herself for being afraid of him. *I won't let him know he scares me!* "If you want clean clothes someone has to pick them up, since you don't."

"You stay out of my room! If I want you here, I will tell you!" He looked down at her with a scowl. Realizing he had better not be too mean to the boss's daughter, he added gruffly, "I will get my things together and put them in the laundry pail – but you stay out of here!" He shoved a bulky canvas bag that was sticking out from under his bunk back against the wall with his foot.

She was still shaking when she went up to tell her mother that Mike would bring his laundry himself.

"What is wrong? Did something upset you?" Her mother looked at her pale face with concern.

"Uh – no." Mike's angry face flashed before her, and Sarah decided she had better not tell Mama just how much he scared her. Her father needed him, and she knew he would fire him if he was told that Mike frightened her. *Why was he so mad anyhow? All I did was go to his room to get his dirty old clothes! You would think he had something I wanted to steal.* She shrugged her shoulders. *I guess I will just stay out of his way from now on.*

They docked early that night so they could reach Watervliet during the daylight hours. Sarah knew that her father had contacted Neil Anderson, the farmer who would keep the mules in his pasture while they went on to New York City. He was going to meet them about noon at Watervliet's dock, just outside the lock.

Sarah wrapped her arms around Minnie's neck as she held her reins at the bottom of the ramp in the bow-stable. "You be a good girl while we are gone, Minnie. Eat lots of good grass and rest. We will be back in ten days."

Minnie whinnied, snuffling softly as she nudged Sarah's blonde braids, and Sarah knew that she understood her.

How can Mike be so mean to her?

"Come on, Squirt, we are waiting for you." She looked up at the top of the steep board and she could see Pa standing there ready to guide Minnie down the ramp to the towpath.

"We are coming." Sarah, sure footed as always, led Minnie up the incline to where her father stood. "The other mules are all unloaded?"

"Yes, they are. Mr. Anderson is here just like he promised." Her father led Minnie to the boarding ramp, and held on to her tail as she started down.

Sarah reached the towpath, and saw that Jack stood between the other two mules, holding their reins as he talked to a tall boy with fair hair. Her uncle Dan was leading Maude up a ramp into Mr. Anderson's flatbed wagon, and Mike was behind him with Molly.

"Are they all going to ride in the wagon?" Sarah watched them tie the first two to the high rail near the driver's seat.

"Yes. It is easier than leading them along." The tall boy answered her. He looked about the same age as her cousin, and he had bright blue eyes. He smiled at her, and she saw that he had two deep dimples, one in each cheek.

For some reason that she didn't understand, she felt her cheeks get hot. She could feel herself blushing! To cover her confusion, she turned to Jack. "Are we going to see where they will be pastured?"

Her cousin grinned, enjoying the sight of her red cheeks – *gosh, I think Sarah has discovered boys!* "No, we saw the pastures before. We will just pick up the mules when we come back. This is Mr. Anderson's son, Teddy. We met last year." He turned to Teddy and added mischievously, "This is my little cousin Sarah's first year on the canal. She is a year younger than me."

Teddy smiled as she looked up at him. "Are you having a good time? Do you like being a canawler?" He was looking her over with interest, and she was suddenly glad she was wearing her blue dress that Mama said made her eyes look bluer.

"I love it! Have you ever made a trip up the canal?"

"No, but I have taken a Packet Boat into New York to the harbor. I would like to try riding on a barge some day."

"Sarah! Tell your pa that I have lunch ready, and ask Mr. Anderson and his son to join us." Mama was leaning over the rail behind them.

"I heard you, Abby." Pa took the reins of the last mule to be loaded.

Sarah felt a little spurt of pleasure, realizing that Teddy was going to stay and visit them for a while more. From the wide grin on his face she thought he liked the idea too.

A few minutes later Jack ran back to his family's barge to tell his mother lunch was ready, and Teddy followed Sarah up the ramp to the *Fairchild I*. Pa and Mr. Anderson were just behind them. As they stepped down onto the deck, Mike came out of the bowstable with a dufflebag slung over his shoulder.

"We should be back in ten days. Meet us here about mid day. Can Dan and I count on you being here?" Pa stopped to speak to him.

"I will be here. Most of my gear is still below. I'll take my wages now." Mike held out a dirty palm for the money that the Captain handed him. As soon as he stuffed it in his pocket, he turned and went quickly to the towpath, not bothering to say good-bye to anyone.

"Surly cuss, isn't he?" Neil Anderson remarked as he watched Mike go up the road.

"I have had hogees that were easier to deal with." Captain Fairweather smiled ruefully. "He just happened to be the first one to apply for the job this year as we were ready to leave. I won't take him on for the next trip." He grinned. "I think we are all going to enjoy the next ten days without him. Let's go down and have some lunch."

Chapter TEN

Leaving the Erie Canal

Abigail had prepared a big mid-day meal and they forgot about Mike as Teddy and his father told them the latest news of Watervliet and Troy. The city of Troy was across the river from them, and Mama said she had bought Pa some dress shirts made there. "I like them because their collars are separate and it makes them easier to launder and iron."

"Troy is known as 'the Collar City' you know." Mr. Anderson smiled and took a big bite of his chicken sandwich.

"Why do they call it that?" Sarah asked.

"Let me tell, Pa." Teddy was eager to impress Sarah. "We learned about it in school. There was this Mrs. Hannah Orlando Montague who made the first shirts with detached collars for her husband, way back in 1819. So many people asked her to make some for them that they started to manufacture them, and they keep getting more and more popular. I have two myself for Sunday wear." He grinned at her, and his dimples deepened. "So, that is why Troy got to be called the 'Collar City'."

"That is amazing!" Sarah gazed at him in open admiration.

Her father chuckled. "Neil tells me that Teddy has never been on a barge. Why don't you and Jack give him a tour of ours before we have to leave?"

The three of them left quickly. They took Teddy down to the bow stable to show him where the mules stayed when they were not walking the towpath.

He wrinkled his nose and laughed. "It smells just like the stable back at our farm."

"While we are being towed down-river we will give it a good cleaning and some fresh hay." Sarah looked around her and realized that she and Jack had a big job ahead of them. Pa had told her that he would give them money to spend in New York City if they did a good job.

"Yeah. Of course it will smell just the same a day or two after the mules come back." Jack laughed.

"What is in there?" Teddy pointed to the door of Mike's room.

"That is where Mike sleeps. We are not supposed to go in there." Sarah frowned, remembering how mad he had been at her.

"He has made sure of that." Jack laughed again as he pointed at the big padlock on the outside of the door. "He must have put that on after he came back from Schenectady."

Before long Mr. Anderson said it was time for him and Teddy to leave. They would have to travel slowly with the load of mules. He promised to meet them again in ten days to return the team to them.

Sarah watched them leave from the deck, and Teddy turned to wave as he and his father started down the road.

"Sarah's got a boyfriend!" Jack teased her.

"I have not!" She could feel her cheeks get hot again. "But he is nice – and he doesn't tease me like you do." She stuck her tongue out at him.

"We are about ready to tie into the tow. I thought we might have time to see a little of Watervliet, but maybe we can on the way back." Pa pulled the landing plank in. "You two would enjoy seeing the Arsenal here. It is the oldest one in the whole country. It was built in 1813, and a lot of weapons are made here."

A small tug attached itself to their barges and pulled them to the point where a line of barges were waiting to make the two day trip into New York City's harbor. It was almost three that afternoon when the line at last was complete and nine barges began the trip behind the steam-powered tug that would take them on their journey.

"Let's all take the rest of the day off and enjoy the sights." Captain Fairweather settled into his seat in the stern with his pipe sending a wreath of smoke above his head. Sarah and Jack, and her mother, joined him to watch the receding shores of Watervliet. Looking across the wide expanse of water, they could see the skyline of Troy.

Sarah drew a deep sigh of pleasure. ***This has been the best day yet! Mike is gone for ten days – the mules don't have to be walked – and I met Teddy Anderson!***

Chapter ELEVEN

New Adventure!

Now that the tug was pulling them everyone relaxed. They were on the Hudson River and there would be no locks to go through. The river was lined with villages who sent Bum Boats out to visit the tugs.

"Why do they call them that, Pa?" Sarah was watching a canopied steam-powered boat that was attaching itself to a tow going down the river ahead of them.

"Because they bum a ride with whatever tow they hitch up to, and they stay with it until it passes a tow going the other way. Tomorrow, we may have one attach itself to our tow and we will go aboard." Her father stretched his arms over his head. "I am really looking forward to this trip!"

"Last year we went aboard a bum boat near Kingston and they sold everything! Fresh ice cream and candy, and all kinds of treats." Jack licked his lips, remembering all the good things he had tried. "Are we going to eat pretty soon?"

"I swear you have a hollow leg, Jack Fairweather!" Abby laughed. "Yes, we will eat in just a little while." She waved to his mother where she sat in the bow of the *Fairchild II* riding almost against their stern. "Is it safe to go back and forth while we are being towed, John?"

"Dan and I made that portable bridge a couple of years ago." Her husband pointed to a long, flat piece of wood almost half the width of the cabin roof. "We made hooks on both boats so we can fasten them on. It comes in handy when we want to go from one boat to another while we are being towed."

"I wondered what that was for." Sarah climbed up to the roof of the cabin and Jack followed her. They sat with their knees bent and looked out at the green hills and tiny houses they could see in the distance.

"Tomorrow morning, when we reach Kingston, we will probably be visited by a bum boat. Until then we have to depend on our own kitchen." The captain grinned at his wife. "Have you still got a few treats left?"

"Enough for tonight, without Mike to feed." She smiled. "That man eats enough for two – and he never had a pleasant word!" She drew a pad and stubby pencil from her apron pocket. " I have to make a list of things we need if we do get a chance to shop."

"The air smells different than it does on the canal." Sarah sniffed. "I like it."

"We are getting into salt water now so it smells like the ocean." Her father smiled. "I would not try drinking it. It would make you sick. And it is not much good for washing clothes. Everything gets rough and crusty. We still have fresh water in the barrels, thank goodness."

"It is great for swimming though! Remember last year we swam when the tow stopped for an hour?" Jack said. "Do you think we might get a chance to swim tomorrow?"

"I would not be surprised. These two days will go by quickly, so enjoy them." Captain Fairweather puffed contentedly on his pipe.

He was right. The next day they reached Kingston just before noon, and as he had predicted, a steam powered boat with a gaily striped awning fastened itself to the hooks that usually fastened the mules tow lines. Sarah and her parents and Jack's family eagerly clambered down onto its decks.

The inside cabin was full of counters with high stools bolted to the floor in front of them. The shelves behind them were full of canawlers needs. Sarah's mother filled her baskets with spices, coffee, flour and sugar. There was fresh milk as well as cookies that smelled so good that Sarah's mouth watered, and candy. Just as Jack remembered, there were tubs of fresh ice cream too.

Two hours went by quickly. Pa and Uncle Dan and two men from other barges who had come across the portable bridges sat at one end of the counter, enjoying the first cold beer of the trip. Abigail and Mabel joined Jack and Sarah eating big bowls of ice cream, and they each chose treats to take back to their barge before the owners of the bum boat said it was time to move forward in the tow.

By the time that they had stowed their purchases, they could see the city of Poughkeepsie along the shoreline, and Pa said that meant they were half-way to the harbor. It was time to do a little work. Sarah and Jack were sent to clean the bow stable and it was late in the day before they finished changing the hay on the floor, cleaning the feed mangers, and shoveling waste overboard. The little closet where the slop pail was kept was scrubbed, and fresh sawdust put on the floor. The two of them stood, hands on hips to survey their finished work. *I smell like Minnie and the other two girls.* Sarah looked at her dirty hands ruefully.

Just before dusk the tow stopped for an hour and most of those who could swim changed into swimming gear. They jumped into the cold, clear water and had their first real bath since leaving home. Sarah and her family had washed in the cabin, but some canawlers who traveled with only the owner and crew had probably not washed all over since they started their trip.

Now, they splashed and floated and soaped themselves liberally as they paddled around their barges. Sarah's mother and father were both good swimmers, and so was she and her cousin. Jack's father jumped in with them, but Aunt Mabel sat by the rail land watched. She preferred her tub in the kitchen galley. The nights were cold on the water, and no one stayed in too long, but the salt water was refreshing and they all felt clean once more.

"We had better get a good night's sleep. Tomorrow we should dock in the harbor and get ready to unload our cargo." Sarah's father tousled her damp hair as she came out of her cuddy in her long nightgown.

"I will never forget this trip! I am so glad you let me come!" She threw her arms around him, and he hugged her tightly.

She was fast asleep almost before she pulled her covers up.

Chapter TWELVE

The Plot Thickens

Sarah was up and ready for the day before the tow arrived at New York City's busy harbor. She had wakened to the sound of other boats near them, and the closer they came to the city, the busier the waters were. There were tugs pushing covered deck barges, moving packaged freight, and open deck barges handling bulk freight. She could see double-ended passenger ferry boats shuttling back and forth across the harbor, delivering people and their cargo to their destinations. Garbage scows were being towed out to sea, where their refuse would be dumped beyond the city limits. Ocean-going freighters were anchored, waiting to be docked at the pier. Sarah watched, fascinated as the small tugs pushed and pulled the big liners into position at the North River Pier.

The tow stopped so Pa and Uncle Dan, with help from warehouse workers, could unload his lumber at the big Steinway piano factory near the Brooklyn Pier. And, as other tugs were emptied of their cargo, they were towed to the piers on South Street at Manhattan Island. Pa said it might be two or three days before he arranged for a load to tow west to Syracuse or maybe even Buffalo. That meant that the family could do some sightseeing!

Sarah and her mother and Aunt Mabel visited the busy Fulton Street fish market, and Sarah's eyes opened wide at the sights and smells. Pushcarts were selling all kinds of things. Mama promised they would buy fresh oysters or clams to take back for supper before they left. She let Sarah try some on the half-shell, even though they cost a penny a piece! When they got hungry, Mama treated her and Aunt Mabel to a Coney Island Red Hot that looked like a long hot dog and tasted like one too.

"These are too costly, Abigail." Aunt Mabel protested weakly, as she eagerly took a big bite of hers. "Imagine! A nickel for a hot dog!"

Abby laughed. "Enjoy it! We might not get back here until next year."

"I wish Jack could have come with us." Sarah licked the mustard from her fingers, and her mother gave her a paper napkin to finish the job.

"It is time for him to start learning the business. He has gone with your pa and Uncle Dan." Abigail raised her parasol to shield her eyes from the bright sun. Sarah thought she looked prettier than any of the other women shopping in the square. Her blonde hair was done in a high pompadour. Sarah had watched, fascinated, as she wrapped it around a big piece of rolled netting and fastened it with long hairpins. Usually, Mama pulled her long hair back into a knot at the nape of her neck. She preferred her parasol to the wide-brimmed hats so many of the women, including Aunt Mabel, wore. Her full skirted dress was the same shade of blue as the one Sarah wore.

When they finished eating, they walked the short distance to the New York City Aquarium in Battery Park. Mama and Aunt Mabel had been there before, but Sarah was enchanted. The aquarium was in a big circular red brick building, and she went from one glass tank to another, gazing at the salt-water fish in each. There were seahorses, dolphins, seals, octopi, swordfish, huge turtles, and so many others that she knew she would never remember all of their names.

"Time to leave, Sarah, if we are to get back in time to prepare supper." Her mother smiled as she saw how reluctant she was to leave. "We still have a few days to enjoy. Maybe we will have time to come back."

When they returned to their barge Pa said there had been a change of plans. He had a broad grin on his face. "We made a deal to haul some sea gravel to Smith's Roofing Company in Tonawanda, and we will be towed tomorrow morning over to Oyster Bay to the gravel beds.

"Does that mean we can't see any more things here?" Sarah could not keep her disappointment from showing.

"No. It means we will go and get loaded and then be towed back here. We will be ready to go, but we will wait for the next tow going back to the Hudson. We will probably have another two or three days to see some of the sights."

Sarah drew a deep breath of relief. "Good! There are so many things to see!"

Jack grinned. "Pa says you can show me all the things I missed today."

"I will!" Sarah started to tell him about some of the fish she had seen in the aquarium, and her mother laughed.

"Let him see for himself when you go back. Right now, both of you need to get into bed."

The next morning a small steam tug hooked up to their barges and towed them up the East River, through the Hell Gate. A few hours later they were pulled on Long Island Sound to Oyster Bay. There they moored at the gravel dock and were ready to load. It took two days to fully load their barges, and Sarah was kept busy helping her mother to ready their cabin for the return trip. They stripped their beds and put on clean linen. Dishes were washed and put back on clean shelves, and the black iron cook stove was polished until it shone once more. Abigail scrubbed the wooden kitchen floor on her knees. They kept a pad handy, and she and Sarah listed all the supplies they would need for the trip back along the canal. While Jack and Sarah went sightseeing she and Aunt Mabel would go shopping.

They arrived back at South Street before noon of the third day, and Pa and Uncle Dan would go to seek out a tow for the return trip.

"You two stay together, and do not go any farther than the aquarium." Sarah's mother nervously tucked Sarah's stray curls back. "Are you sure you know the way? Have you got the money your papa gave you?"

Sarah giggled. "Yes, Mama." She held out the little purse that contained the coins Papa had given her. "We will be careful, and we will be back to meet you before supper time." She was almost dancing with excitement. She couldn't wait to get started.

Jack jingled his money in his town-pants pockets. "Pa loaned me his pocket watch so we can be sure to come back before you are ready to go back to the barge. Come on, Sarah." He took her hand and pulled her towards the Fulton Market.

"Whew! I thought sure they were going to make us stay with them!" He grinned. "Okay, cuz, lead on. What do we see first?"

"Let's have a hot dog. We can eat it on our way over to the aquarium. And we can stop and see the Brooklyn Bridge, and the Statue of Liberty on our way." Sarah gave an exuberant little skip, as she kept up with Jack's long stride.

They leaned together against a railing as they ate their hot dogs, dripping with mustard, and gazed out towards the harbor where they could see scows and barges being moved from one dock to another by the little steam tugs that were so much smaller that the boats they moved.

"Isn't that awesome?" Sarah demanded.

For once Jack could not do anything but agree with her,

and, a little later as they looked at the impressive structure of the nearby bridges, they had to stop until he absorbed their beauty. Before they turned to go he said, "Some day I am going to learn how to build things like that." His face was solemn, and he had a determined look on his usually carefree face as he cranked his neck to see some of the tall buildings around them.

They entered the round red building that held the aquarium. It was cool and dim after the bright sun outside, and they paused in the open lobby to look around. Suddenly, Sarah grasped Jack's arm. "Look over there! Isn't that Mike?" She nodded towards the soaring rounded tank where some of the larger fish were swimming.

The tank was across the big room, and it took Jack a minute to follow her gaze. "You are right! But, who is he talking to? And how did he get here?" Jack took a step in that direction and Sarah pulled him back.

"Don't let him see you!" She pulled on his sleeve until he backed around the corner where Mike could not see them. They both peered cautiously around the tank, and watched as Mike stood deep in conversation with another man. They were dressed in black jackets with brown trousers tucked into scruffy boots. Mike's friend had straggly red hair and a scruffy red beard. They were so involved in what they were talking about that they paid no attention to anyone in the crowded lobby.

"Crimeny! That guy kind of looks like Mike, doesn't he?" Jack leaned out farther to get a good look.

"Yes. He does. Maybe it is his brother?" Sarah was puzzled. "What is Mike doing here, Jack? We left him way back in Watervliet."

"I don't know." Jack pushed his hands through his dark, curly hair. "I wonder if this means he won't be going back with us when we get back to the canal?"

The plot thickens.

They watched the two men for another few minutes, until they suddenly headed in their direction, going towards the doors to the street. Sarah drew Jack farther back where they would not see them, and they watched until they went out the door.

"What do you think of that?" Jack was puzzled. "If he wanted to come to the city, why didn't he just ride with us?"

"I don't know what to think. You know what?" Sarah's eyes widened in excitement. "That man matched the description of the bank robber! I will bet Mike is working with him."

"That's a crazy idea! Mike has been on the barge all the way down from Rome. How could he be mixed up in a bank robbery?"

"Maybe." She felt a little foolish. "Well, let's look at the fish."

For the rest of the afternoon though she kept remembering those men. And she could not shake the feeling that red headed man might be the bank robber. *I'm going to tell Papa about what we saw and see what he thinks.*

Chapter THIRTEEN

Leaving the City

Supper that night was exciting. Papa and his brother had arranged for a tow to pick them up the next day.

"They will pick us up about noon with a harbor tug and tow us up the North River near Fifty-second Street where we will be tied to the stake boat that is anchored in the middle of the river. We will have to stay aboard because we will leave when the tide has swung us into position. I hope you all saw as much as you could today."

"I am ready to go. I think I bought everything that could possibly fit into my cupboards." Abby laughed. "How about you, Sarah?"

"I could stay longer. There is so much to see. But, I'll be glad to see Minnie, Maude and Molly again. We will come back again, won't we?"

"Probably many times. At least as long as the Erie Canal continues to operate and I have lumber to haul, and orders to fill." The Captain's face was sober for a moment. "Some of the canawlers I talked to while we have been here tell me that the demand for canal travel is becoming lighter because of the trains that are hauling freight and people."

His brother grinned. "But, didn't they tell us too that the trains are unreliable? Their coal power keeps them in constant danger of fire. There are still a lot of passengers who would like to go by train because it is a little faster, but the danger from flying sparks, and the dirt, make them continue to use the canal and the Packet Boats."

"True. I hear there are two Packet Boats operating between here and Albany that offer a good ride and they are full night and day. Captain John smiled. "I didn't mean that I thought we would be closing down any time soon."

"Pa, Jack and I saw Mike at the Aquarium today with another man who kind of looked like Mike, except he had red hair – you know like the bank robber we heard about?"

Her father burst out laughing. "Sarah, you have the most vivid imagination of anyone I know! Are you sure it was Mike? We left him back in Watervliet."

"It was him, Uncle John." Jack agreed with Sarah. "And he was with a man who looked just like Sarah says. Of course I don't see how they could be working together. Mike has been on board our barges ever since we left Rome. I've been trying to tell her that."

"Well, we will have to see if he gets back to Watervliet in time to join us, if it was him. Captain John frowned. "It will leave us short-handed if he does not show up."

"We could find someone else, couldn't we? I almost hope he does not decide to go back with us." Abigail frowned. "I can't remember when I have met a meaner tempered man."

"He will be back." Sarah declared. "He has a big padlock on his room and he said no one was to go in there because he left most of his stuff there."

"Time will tell, I guess. Right now I think we had better get a good night's sleep. Tomorrow will be another busy day."

The next morning everything went just as the Captain had predicted. The harbor tug took them out to the almost fully loaded tow, and before night fell they were ready to start back towards Albany and Watervliet.

Early in the morning they passed by Riverside Park and caught a glimpse of its grandeur, where it could be seen close to the shoreline. A few miles outside of New York they saw the beginning of the Palisades, rocky cliffs that could be seen for miles on the New Jersey shore near the west side of the Hudson River. Before they reached the end of them, they had passed Yonkers, Dobbs Ferry, Tarrytown and Rockland Lake – all places Sarah had heard about but never seen. She had started a journal of this trip down the canal and she scribbled furiously, making sure the names of the places they passed were spelled right.

Late that afternoon Pa called her up to sit with him on the deck so he could show her the towers of Sing Sing Prison. He told her how his father had told him about this place where hardened criminals who had committed murders were put to death.

Sarah shivered, picturing what that must feel like.

Just before dark, they passed West Point Military Academy in plain view on this west side of the river. Her book was becoming full! They were still under way when she fell asleep that night.

The next morning, they had reached the half-way point of Poughkeepsie. She was up on deck in time to see the only bridges crossing the Hudson River between Albany and New York. One was the railroad bridge crossing to Highland. Pa pointed out a lighthouse at Roundout Creek called the Esopus Light. He said the lighthouse beacon had guided tows entering the creek at night for years. "When we get this far, I know we are getting close to Albany." He stretched and tapped the ashes from his pipe. "Tomorrow, we will be picking up the mules."

Chapter FOURTEEN

Back on the Canal

The next morning they were towed past Kingston and found themselves once more in fresh water. Sarah's father pointed out the Knickerbocker Ice Company's ice houses where blocks of ice could be purchased to fill their steel boxes and let them keep meat and milk fresh longer. A Bum Boat came along just as he was telling her. It was owned by the ice company and Mama and Aunt Mabel took the chance to fill their boxes, and buy fresh vegetables and fruit from another Bum Boat that closely followed the first one.

Sarah munched a crisp apple as she sat on the roof of the cabin with Jack, watching the shoreline slip by.

"It will not be long before you will not be able to sit up there." Her father warned them. "Once we are locked into the canal we will be seeing low bridges again."

The sun was high in the sky when they approached Albany and Rensselaer, on opposite sides of the Hudson River. A tug pulled them and the other canal barges who did not want to wait in Albany's busy harbor on to Watervliet.

As they approached the harbor Sarah's sharp eyes found Teddy Anderson's tall figure on the shore. He saw her too, and waved vigorously. She fancied she could see his wide smile and his dimples. "Look, Pa! There is Teddy, and there are our mules."

"You are right." The Captain joined her at the rail, and

her mother came hurrying up from the galley. Jack came nimbly across their little bridge and jumped down to the deck.

"Pa wants to know, do you want to unlatch the bridge and stow it?"

"I guess we had better." The Captain waved to his brother. In just a short time they had disconnected the big plank and put it back on the cabin roof.

They drew into the shore and their escort dropped them off. With a brief wave, the pilot of the small steam powered tug turned and headed back to the middle of the river. They were ready to relock into the canal again.

The landing ramp landed on the towpath and Sarah was there to scamper down to the ground. Her legs felt shaky on firm ground after so long on the water, but she smiled at Teddy as he came running over to the barge. His father was just behind him.

"Hello! We thought you would be along this afternoon." Teddy's blue eyes were bright and he looked happy to see them.

Sarah could feel her cheeks getting warm again. "I was surprised when I saw you waiting." She hesitated, not knowing what to say next. "Um, how are the mules?"

"They are good. My pa is getting ready to help you load them." Her father and uncle and Jack had gone on to the wagon where the mules had all been tied to the tailgate, waiting for them. She had been so excited to see Teddy again that she had not noticed that they had gone ahead of them.

"Your hogee is here too. My pa tried to talk to him, but he is not too friendly." Teddy grinned.

"Mike is here? We saw him in New York City. I didn't think he would make it back here in time." She giggled. "I was kind of hoping that he wouldn't."

"There he is." Teddy pointed to a building at the back of the dock where they sold beer and whiskey. Sarah saw Mike come towards them. He carried a big canvas duffel slung over his shoulder and he paused only a minute before mounting the landing ramp.

"Tell your pa I'm unloading my gear in my room and I will be right back." He was not any friendlier than he had been before leaving them.

"I saw you in New York. How did you get back?" Sarah blurted the words before she could stop herself.

"You did not see me in New York. I have been right around here waiting for you." He swung around on his heel, his face red, and then hurried up the plank and dropped onto the deck.

"He is lying. Jack and I both saw him in the aquarium in New York City." Sarah shook her head in disbelief, and turned as Pa and Jack came near with the first two mules.

"Didn't I just see Mike going aboard?" Her father raised a dark eyebrow.

"You did. He says he was not in New York." She was indignant.

"Let's not worry about it right now. We need to get loaded and into the lock before it gets dark." He looked anxiously at the darkening sky.

"We need to get a start back to the farm as soon as we can too." Neil Anderson agreed as he joined them, leading the last mule.

Mike came down onto the tow path just then, and Captain Fairweather greeted him cordially. "How was the vacation, Mike?"

"Okay, I guess." His face was surly. "I suppose you want me to take the first shift?"

"Yes. Why don't you harness Minnie while we load the others into the bow stable. It looks like we won't have a delay getting into the lock."

They worked smoothly and all too soon they were ready to board. Sarah hated to say good-bye to Teddy so quickly, and he shuffled his feet nervously before he reached into his pocket and took out a folded paper. "It's my address. Would you want to write me a letter when you have time?"

She looked up at him shyly, and nodded. "Just a minute." She ran up the ramp and grabbed her journal from the roof of the cabin where she had left it. She put her name and address on a page and ripped it out of the book before she ran back to give it to him. "In case you want to write too, I won't be home for a while, but we could both write and I would have a letter waiting when we get home."

His face lit up with a grin. "That is a great idea. I'll do it. Don't forget!"

"I won't." She saw that they were ready to go, and Teddy's father called to him. "Time to go, son."

Reluctantly, she climbed the ramp and her father pulled it in. Teddy waved once more and turned to go with his father. Pa chuckled. *I do believe my little girl is growing up!* He called to Mike where he stood next to Minnie on the path.

Within a short time they had been locked into the lock at Watervliet, and Mike was on his way to meet them on the other side. Going to the bow as the gates swung open, Sarah saw that they were low in the lock, the walls high above them. *Oh, I forgot Pa said we would be raised eight feet or more in each lock until we reach that level stretch into Rome.*

By the time that they reached the other side of the lock they had been raised almost to the top of the walls. Her stomach churned from the upward movement, and then they were gently swelled out of the gates into the canal. Turning, she could see Uncle Dan's boat right behind them, following true on his towline. The mules were reattached and they were on their way again.

Chapter FIFTEEN

Sarah Takes a Bold Step

The next morning was bright and clear. The air was warm and fresh and Sarah thought that she could smell some of the summer flowers along the berm side of the canal. She had grown accustomed now to the way the canal curved with the towpath on one side, and the berm, the tall banks that made up that part of the wall on the opposite side. Bridges so low that barges sometimes lost some cargo that had been piled too high were spaced at intervals as they floated West.

Often, when a bridge was reached, the towpath would switch to the opposite side on the far side of the bridge and the other side would become the berm. When that happened, the hogee walking the mules would guide them across the bridge, holding their lines up so they would not get tangled, and continue walking as the barge floated through. Pa had explained to her that the bridges were put in by New York State when the canal was dug, and they divided farmer's lands in the process, so they built the bridges for the farmers to go from one part of their farm to another. They spent the state's money grudgingly and that was why they made the bridges so low. It cost less if they did not have to use more material on a higher bridge. As a result, barges that floated under empty, high in the water, risked hitting the bridge abutments. That was one reason most canawlers tried to haul freight both ways. Of course it was more profitable too. Captain Fairweather told her that the expression, *Low Bridges, High Water, Everybody Down* that she had heard canawlers quote so often was a result of their frustration with the state for making their lives more difficult.

This morning Jack was walking the mules and Pa moved the barge close enough to the towpath so she could jump down to join him. She brought him some of the doughnuts Abigail had fried just a few minutes before, and he wolfed them down, smacking his lips.

"Those were great! I was starving." He wiped his greasy hands on his trousers.

"You are always starving." She laughed, and then she became serious. "I wanted to tell you about Mike reading my journal when he was alone in the galley. Mama says he told her he can't read, but I had written Teddy a letter telling him about seeing Mike in New York, and I told him I thought he was working with the bank robber. He was holding my book in his hand when I went down, and he was meaner than ever."

"That was a dumb thing to do, but if he can't read, what difference does it make?" Jack tousled her hair teasingly. "How does it feel to have a boyfriend? I never thought I would see the day Sarah Fairweather would admit that she liked a boy!"

"He is just a friend!" She could feel her cheeks redden. "But he is nice. There is something else, Jack. I peeked into Mike's room yesterday while he was on the towpath, and I saw that he has two big canvas bags under his bunk instead of the one he had before we dropped him in Watervliet. What if he has some of the robber's money in one of them?"

"You are too much! How did you have nerve enough to go into his room after the last time?" He looked at her in surprise. "Did you open the bags?"

She shook her head. Mama called me, so I didn't have time."

"You had better stay out of there. He might really hurt you if he catches you." Jack looked concerned.

"I know, but we are getting closer to home every day. What if he has money in there and we let him get away with it?"

Jack shrugged. "We are just kids. No one pays any attention to us when we try to tell them anything. I don't think there is anything you can do about it."

"Well, I am going to if I get the chance." She was determined.

For the first time in his life, Jack thought that she looked like her father when he had made his mind up to something. He had always thought she was just like his Aunt Abigail.

When Mike took his turn on the towpath with Minnie that afternoon, Pa had just told Sarah that they were almost into Fonda. They would reach Utica the next day. She was running out of time!

She went down to clean the bowstable while he was on the towpath, and spread clean hay. She filled the mangers with oats, but she kept looking at Mike's door. The padlock was not on it. No one was down here but her. She could not stop looking at that door! Maybe it was locked, even though she could not see a padlock. *Maybe I will just try the knob.* It turned easily in her hand, and almost on its own, swung open. The smell of dirty clothes hit her sharply, and she held her breath as she stepped just inside.

The bed was unmade as always, and both of those canvas bags stuck out from under it. Still holding her breath, she crept over and knelt next to the bed. She reached out to poke the closest bag. It felt bumpy, but kind of soft – like it was full of clothes. Disappointed, she reached for the other bag. It was shoved back a little more, and when she tentatively pulled on the closed top of it, it was heavy. She pulled on the first one and it came out easily. She loosened the tie and peeked in. She could see some of Mike's shirts, rolled and stuffed in carelessly. She retied the string. She took a deep breath and gave a good tug on the other bag. It moved out enough so that she could untie the heavy thong holding it shut. She hesitated, then quickly pulled it open. A package of money, held together by a paper band, slid out onto the floor. *I was right!*

She reached in and pulled out a handful of banded money, then peered inside the bag. It looked like it was full of money! Quickly, she shoved it all back inside the bag and pulled the thong tight again, shoving it back under the bed. Her mind was whirling as she sat back on her heels. "I have to tell Pa." She went to the bow stable and headed for the ramp. Just as she reached the top there was a terrific splash just in front of the barge. The boat rocked, and Maude and Molly brayed loudly in their stalls, as she heard the dreaded words – "Mule In The Canal!"

Minnie survives a fall into the canal!

Chapter SIXTEEN

Mule in the Canal

When she heard that cry – "Mule In The Canal!" she ran to the bow. It was Minnie! Sarah ran to the landing plank.

"Cut her loose!" Captain John yelled as he tied off his tiller and ran to jump down to the towpath. Mike stood perfectly still, the end of a long rein in his hand. The captain ran by him, yanking the reins from him as he dove into the water. His brother followed him, and Jack came running as Sarah reached the towpath. Minnie was wildly thrashing, her heavy harness dragging her down under the water. She had gone under twice and fought her way back to the surface, but she was tiring. She was so frightened that she fought the two men's efforts to calm her until they finally got her heavy harness off. Without that awful weight, they started to float her close to the edge of the canal. She brayed weakly, and rolled her eyes, still thrashing the water with her feet. Captain John got his head under her chin and kept her head above water as his brother pushed her towards an escape hole just a few feet away from them.

Another barge that had approached from the other direction saw what had happened and drew close just the other side of the escape hole.

One of the men jumped into the water, which fortunately was only about eight feet deep on this stretch of the canal. He swam to the escape hole and climbed onto the bank.

Abigail had reached the towpath, and when she saw Jack trying to lift the top to the escape hole with Sarah, she snapped at Mike – who was still standing so still he looked frozen. "Mike get over there and help the children lift that cover! Now!"

Her sharp tone seemed to wake him from his daze and he shuffled forward, but before he got there the man from the other barge had reached them, and he helped them to lift the heavy planking. Between them they turned it over and slid the cleated side down into the opening that had been dug into the side of the canal for emergencies like this. It made a rough ramp for the mule. As Jack jumped down into the escape hole, Minnie scrambled up into the opening. As she felt firm footing, she seemed almost calm and she awkwardly climbed the ramp back to the towpath where she could see Sarah waiting for her. Sarah pulled her the last feet by her bridle. Minnie gained the towpath and shook herself mightily. Out of the corner of her eyes she spotted Mike, and she reared. He jumped back and she stretched her neck trying to reach him.

"Get her away! She's crazy!" Mike backed away from the agitated mule.

"Whoa girl, whoa." Captain Fairweather crooned to her as he climbed to the top too. Finally, between him and Sarah, she quieted and twitched her ears, lowering her head for Sarah's soothing strokes. *He almost killed me!* The canawler who had come to their aid was an old-timer who had ridden the canal for many years. His shrewd blue eyes had watched Minnie's actions when she spotted Mike. He rubbed his grizzled beard thoughtfully. "I'd have me a careful look at that there mule. She acts to me like she's been hurt. How did this happen?"

John Fairweather's face was grim. "I aim to find out. Thank you for your help. We have been very lucky. Minnie would have been an awful loss. Can I pay you for your trouble?"

"Not necessary. Glad I was here. Like I said, I would have a good look at her." He looked down at his dripping clothes, and grinned. "Guess I won't need no bath this week!" He helped Captain Dan replace the escape hole cover before he went back to his own barge. "Whoever thought to put these holes in the towpath saved many a canawler's bacon when they are able to save their mules." He shook hands with Dan and left.

It was not long before they brought a shaken Minnie back to her stall in the bow stable. *You don't know how lucky you were that Mike didn't walk with you today! He pushed me in!* She shook herself again as she looked over at her sisters. Sarah reached for a soft towel and started to dry her coat. *That feels good!*

Sarah's father came down the ramp, and looked over at the door to Mike's room. He had gone in and closed the door before they brought Minnie down.

"She's got some cuts where the harness caught on her, and she has a big bruise on her front shoulder, Pa." Sarah was worried. "Is she going to be all right?" Minnie whinnied and nuzzled her shoulder before she lowered her head to her manger full of oats. *I'm really hungry! It must be from all that swimming.*

"You go up and help your Ma. I'll take care of her now." Sarah's father went to the cupboard where he kept ointments for the mules and took out a big round tin. "Go on now. I want to have a private talk with Mike."

She left reluctantly, wondering what he wanted to talk to Mike about that he did not want her to hear.

The supper table was set before he came up from the bow stable and his face was sober.

"Mike will be leaving us in Rome. He denies it, but I am sure he has been abusing Minnie and the other mules. That bruise on her shoulder is not from just one blow. I think he has been hitting her whenever he handles her when we are not around. I almost think he might have done something to force her off the towpath, but I can't prove it. I told him I won't take any more chances with him."

"I know Minnie hates him. She tries to bite him whenever she gets near him." Sarah was solemn. "When will we get to Rome?"

"We should get there tomorrow if we get an early start. It is not too far now. Dan is going to get out our extra harness. It would take too much time to try and dive for what we cut off from Minnie. Once we drop Mike we will pick up Jack's friend Jerry. Jack says he thinks his folks will let him go with us. He is a big lad, and we will make out okay."

"Thank goodness! Supper is ready. Is Mike coming up here to eat? Jack go and tell your Ma and your Pa we are ready." Abby bustled around the galley setting steaming dishes on the table.

"I will take Mike down a plate. I don't think you would want him at your table tonight – he is surly and disagreeable – worse than ever." Her husband filled a plate as he spoke.

His brother and his wife came in and sat at the table as Captain John came back, and Dan approved of his plan to drop Mike in Rome. "I will take Molly on the last walk tonight. The sooner we get rid of that hogee the happier we will all be."

Everyone was quiet as they ate, and Sarah decided as she looked around at their sober faces that she would wait until tomorrow to tell her father about her discovery in Mike's room.

They tied up outside of Ilion that night along a deserted stretch of the canal and left their lanterns burning for any barge that might be traveling past before morning.

72

Chapter SEVENTEEN

Minnie to the Rescue

The next morning Jack took the first walk. They decided to let Minnie rest for another six hours, so he took Maude. After Sarah finished her chores she went to sit next to her father.

He looked at her quizzically, with one black eyebrow raised. "Something on your mind, Squirt?"

She lowered her eyes. "I did something you are not going to like, but I have to tell you about it."

"I'm listening." His voice was quiet.

"Just before everything happened yesterday, I went into Mike's room when he was outside." She looked up at him and said in a rush, "I looked under his bed and I opened one of his canvas bags. It is full of wrapped up money." She looked him in the eye. "Honest, Papa!"

"Say that again!" The Captain sat up straight in his chair.

"It's true. Really! I knew he met that robber in New York, and I saw him bring that big bag back with him. He has two bags down there now instead of just his duffel. So…I looked inside it and it is stuffed full of money." She looked at him almost defiantly.

"God love us! Sarah, go and get your mother and bring her up here!" As she got up obediently, he added, "Don't tell her anything. Just bring her up here where we can talk without being overheard."

Her mother was in the middle of rolling out pie crust,

but seeing Sarah's face, she asked no questions. She wiped her hands and followed her up to the deck. "What is it, John? What is wrong?" She was puzzled as she looked from one sober face to the other.

"Tell her, Sarah."

Taking another deep breath, she told her mother. "I knew it was wrong, Mama, but I just know he has been helping that other man who looks like him, except he has red hair, and I just know he has been robbing those banks we heard about. That is where he got all that money. One of the packages has the name of a bank in Herkimer on the band. I am sorry – but I just had to look!"

Her mother burst out laughing.

Sarah looked at her in amazement. She was laughing?

"Every one says you are like me, Sarah, but you are just like your father! You just cannot resist a mystery!" She saw how Sarah and her husband were both looking at her, and she laughed again. "Well, what are we going to do about this?" She glanced up at her husband. "You think she is right, don't you?"

He chuckled and nodded. "So many things fit together now that I think about it. The times Mike has been away from the boat, or we have been away, and he has been here. And of course there is the money." He laughed again. "I certainly don't pay him enough to have bags full of money."

"But what can we do?" Sarah looked worried.

"I think our best bet is to wait until we are ready to dock in Rome, and face him with it. We will have to hold him until we can get the police – unless he has some good explanation for the money." He looked at his daughter. "You are sure it was real money? A whole bag full?"

"I'm sure," she said firmly.

It was a long day. Mike never came out of his room. Captain John told his brother about their discovery and he agreed they should just watch him until they reached Rome. One of them could go for the police while they were docking so they could take him into custody. Jack walked all afternoon, but he could hardly wait to get to Rome. They didn't want to take a chance that Mike would discover that they knew about the money until it was time, so no one went near him.

As their barge approached the city limits and they neared their docking spot in Rome, Captain John gave his wife the tiller, and told Jack to bring Minnie up from the bow stable. He didn't want her there when he faced Mike. Jack went down and led her up to the deck.

"Hold her reins, Sarah, and stay up here with your mother. I am going down and talk to Mike. Jack, you go and tell your father, and then run up and bring the constable as quick as you can."

"I think Mike is coming up right now!" Jack looked over his uncle's shoulder, and sure enough, Mike was coming up the ramp from the bow stable with one bag under his arm and the other slung over his shoulder.

"Go now Jack! And run!" Captain Fairweather faced Mike as he reached the deck. "Just a minute, Mike. When you came on board you had one duffel bag. Now you have two. I would like to see what you have in them before you leave my barge. I want to make sure what you have is your property." Mike was heavier than him, but he faced him unafraid.

"Sure, Captain." Mike dropped the bag under his arm and took off the one on his shoulder, but instead of releasing it, he swung it hard at the Captain. Sarah was standing near the landing plank with Minnie, and he came right for her. Minnie lunged and hit his shoulder as he neared her, crowding him against the rail. The Captain recovered his balance and grabbed Mike from behind just as his brother bounded up the ramp. Jack had yelled to him where he was going before he left.

"Here, Minnie, I think we have this under control!" Sarah's uncle laughed as he saw his brother sitting on Mike's back where he had landed when he knocked him down. Minnie stood with her feet planted firmly next to Mike. *He is not going any where!* She brayed loudly every time he moved. It was only a few minutes before Jack arrived with Constable Murphy, and it took a few more minutes for Mike to confess that the money in his bag was indeed the money from all the bank robberies along the canal route. He admitted that he had met his partner, who turned out to be his brother, just as Sarah had suspected, whenever he had money to hide. They planned to meet here with the loot today. He glared at Sarah and Minnie as they stood side by side while he talked to the policeman, and the constable congratulated Sarah for discovering Mike's secret stash.

The constable took him away then, but he asked them to arrange to stay overnight in Rome so he could talk to them the next day. The next morning he came to tell them that Mike's brother had shown up just as he said he would, and he was taken into custody too. The constable was a genial Irishman, and he patted Sarah's blonde head approvingly. "There is a reward of one hundred dollars for the capture of these men, and it will be yours."

"Mine? It should really by Minnie's!" She laughed, but then she had an awful thought. "I don't have to stay here to get it, do I? We have only been out on the canal for a few weeks. We have a long way to go and I can't miss that! Can it wait until I come back?"

He laughed. "I think we can arrange to wait until you come back at the end of the season."

"Not the end of the season, Constable. She will be back in time for school." Her mother smiled gently, but Sarah knew she meant it.

"Oh well, we have a long time before that! Wait until I write to Teddy!"